D1203602

PROFESSOR CLARK

THE SCIENCE SHARK®

PRESENTS:

THE ARTS AND SCIENCES OF THE OCEANS

South Florida Science Center and Aquarium

Science Dept. Professor Clark

SCIENCE NOTES

WWW.PROFESSORCLARKTHESCIENCESHARK.COM

Published by Professor Clark the Science Shark
2433 Hope Lane
Palm Beach Gardens, FL 33410
www.ProfessorClarktheScienceShark.com

Book layout by SuOakes Graphic Design, Lake Worth, FL
www.suoakesdesign.com

Printed in the United States of America
ISBN: 978-1-5136-0567-8

Book 3, **The Encounter**, is dedicated to the memory of Andrew "Red" Harris. We will build the reefs and your legacy and make sure you are never forgotten.
-Your loving family, Scott, Martha, Christina and Ryan Harris

Make sure you visit us at our educational website and on social media!

www.ProfessorClarktheScienceShark.com

Instagram: @professorclarkthescienceshark

Facebook: https://www.facebook.com/ProfessorClark

Professor Clark the Science Shark here, sharing another exciting chapter of my life. "The Encounter" is very special to me because it is about my research and my encounters with humans! You land lovers are a strange species. I have to learn more about you.

The crisis of our ecosystems becomes evident more and more every day. I need to find out what is happening and how we can help. Could I bring humans into my aquatic world to help solve the complex problems that our oceans face? Are humans the problem or part of the solution?

As you remember, my first encounter with the little boy was when I was just a shark pup. I thought, "What a strange subject he was!" He frightened me, as I did him, yet there was a close connection. Could I find him again? Could the boy be part of the solution, and what role would his cherished lure play in my life?

The coral reefs, which were my home, are now covered in algae. My poor reefs are in terrible trouble. Is it like this in other parts of the world's oceans? This is where I need help from you, land lovers. Together we can teach and guide the next generation about the importance of our oceans and how they play such an intricate part of our well-being, our livelihood, and our existence. As you will see in this chapter, with help from my friends maybe we still have time to Save our Seas!

So, come swim on this journey with my friends and me and see how we can begin to make a difference. We will all learn together to help educate the next generation!

Fincerely,
Professor Clark The Science Shark

Professor Clark the Science Shark just couldn't seem to *relax* since returning to his familiar reef off the Jupiter, Florida coastline. Night after night, Clark swam back and forth from one reef to another.

I CAN'T RELAX...

"You are making me very dizzy!" his friend Ray the Remora grumbled, as he tried to get comfortable on Clark's broad tiger shark back.

Clark knew why he couldn't relax! The coral reefs locally, and possibly worldwide, were in trouble, and the young science shark needed to discover solutions to fix them before it was too late!

As Clark looked around at his aquatic playground, he wondered, "What could be responsible for the oceans' problems? Could it be that humans are involved with all of the **reef pollution** and neglect?"

To understand the humans' actions and motives, Professor Clark knew he would need to study humans much closer than ever before!

Professor Clark lived on a reef close to Florida's east coast next to the **Gulf Stream waters**. This ideal location gave him some amazing opportunities to observe the humans while he remained quiet and unseen.

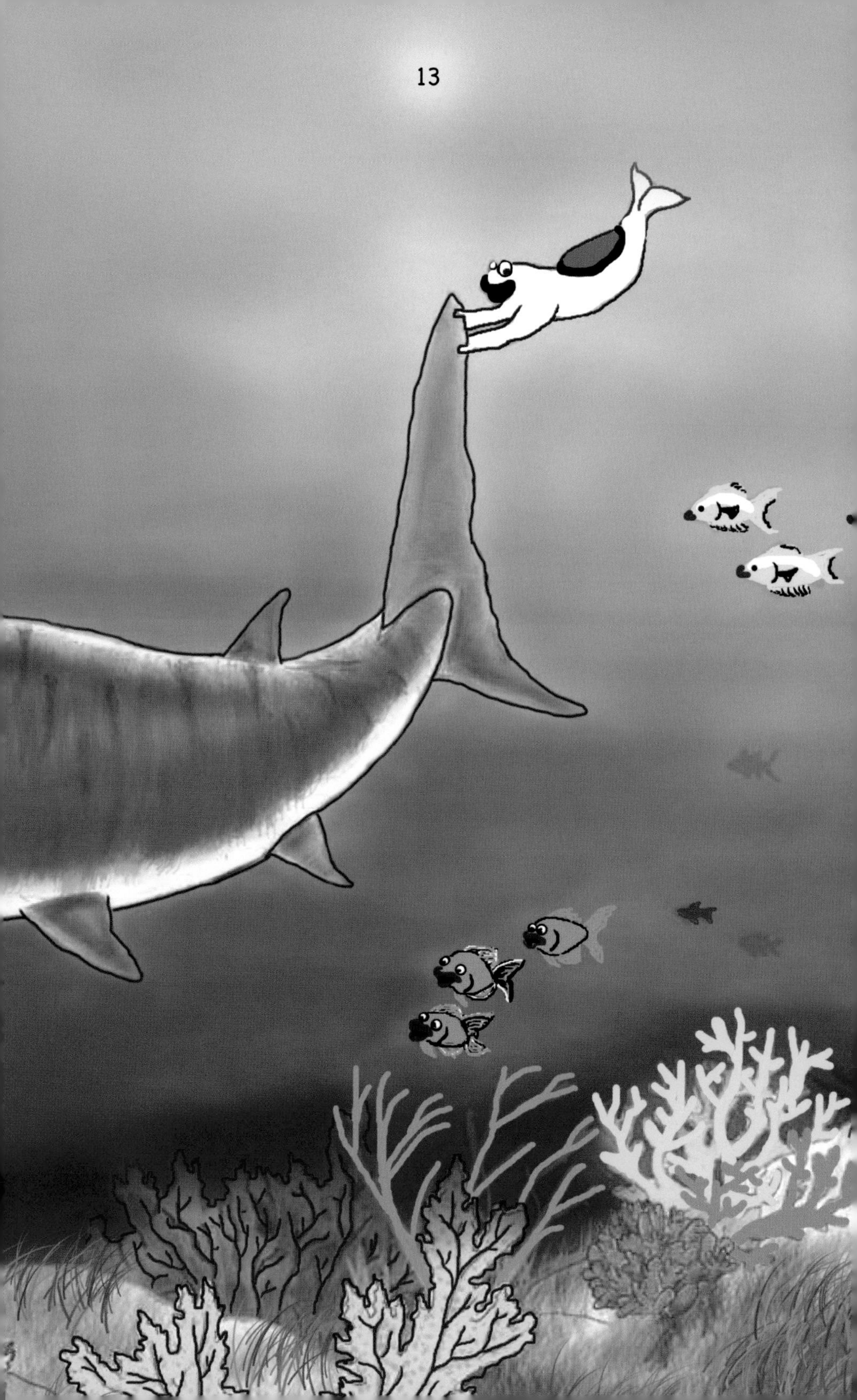

Early the next morning, Professor Clark and Ray set off on another seafaring adventure to study man more closely! The two friends didn't have to swim very far before they felt certain vibrations in the water. This could only mean one thing ...humans!

As the two friends looked from afar, Clark felt both awe and amusement as he studied the clumsy humans in their funny looking skin. "What odd looking creatures," he said out loud as he slowly turned and swam away. "They are called *scuba divers*," Ray explained, trying to catch up to Clark.

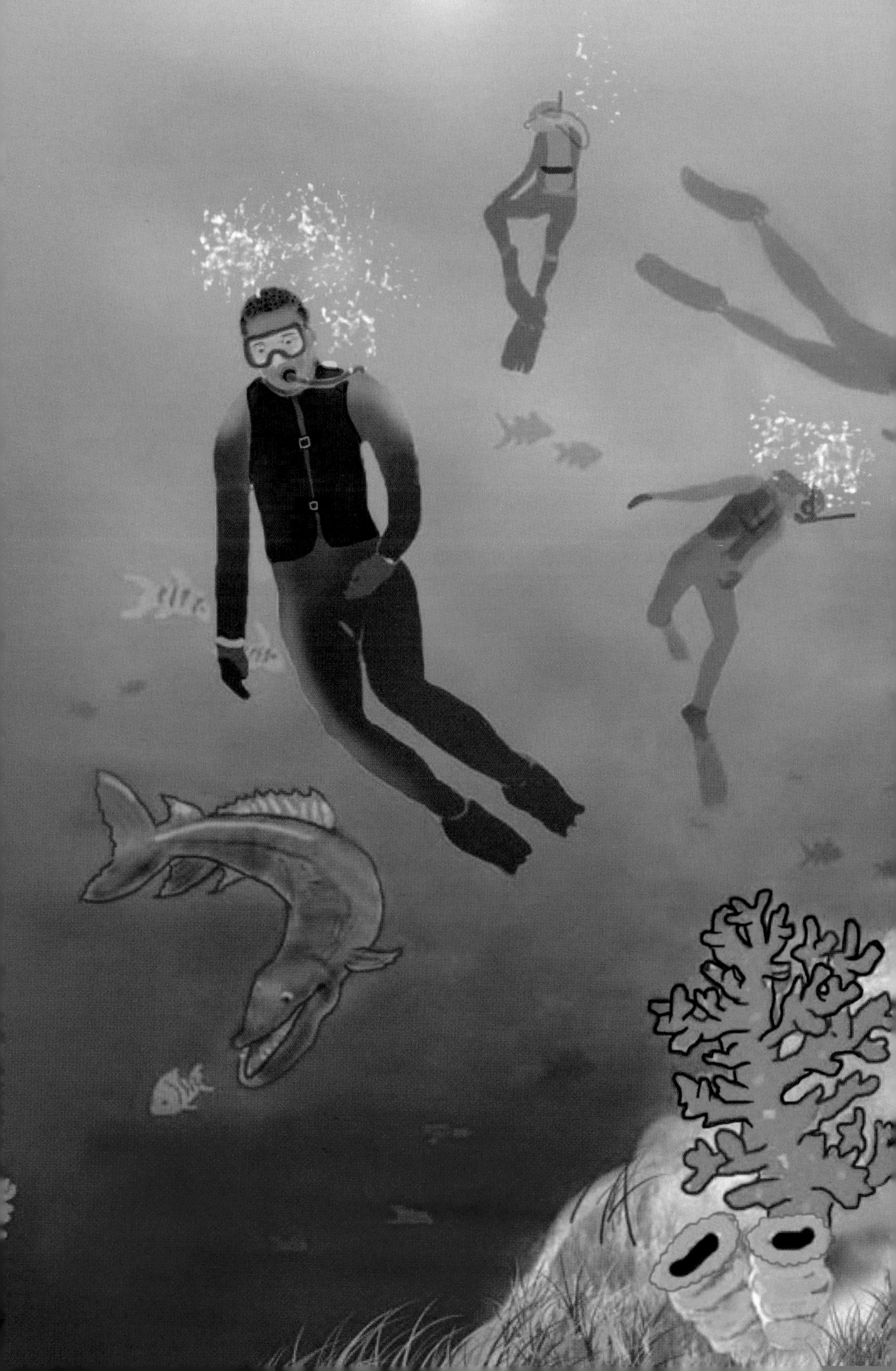

In the coming days, many divers spotted the tiger shark and remora. The interactions didn't always turn out the way Clark had hoped. Many divers were terrified and swam away! Thankfully, many were also fascinated and marveled at Professor Clark's beauty with respect and awe!

Clark and Ray could not understand how anybody could be so frightened by animals they knew so little about. Although he could never be sure which reactions to expect, these encounters helped Professor Clark become more comfortable studying the humans in their **marine environment**. But he wanted more. In his heart he longed to bond with a human!

"Ray," Professor Clark said to his friend, "For some strange reason, I want to get to know these humans and form a friendship with them. It just might solve the oceans' problems!"

Ray didn't know what to say, and it took a few moments before he blurted out, "Are you crazy, Clark? This is a bad idea, a really bad idea!" Ray shouted as he shook his head.

As fate would have it, a young man named Andrew was scuba diving with a couple of friends one morning on Clark and Ray's favorite reef. This was the same human Clark met all those years ago when he was just a little shark pup and Andrew was just a little boy!

Andrew had visited the reef on a regular basis, hoping to find his cherished lure. He also had a secret dream of meeting up with the shark pup one day.

Professor Clark was also hanging around the reef that morning! He knew there were divers ahead by the **electric pulses** in the water. Slowly and cautiously he made his way toward the dark floating objects, only to discover that Andrew was one of those divers!

Clark stopped in his fin
tracks but did not know why.
His mind was racing wildly.
"Can it be?" he asked himself
as he swam slowly toward
the oncoming divers.

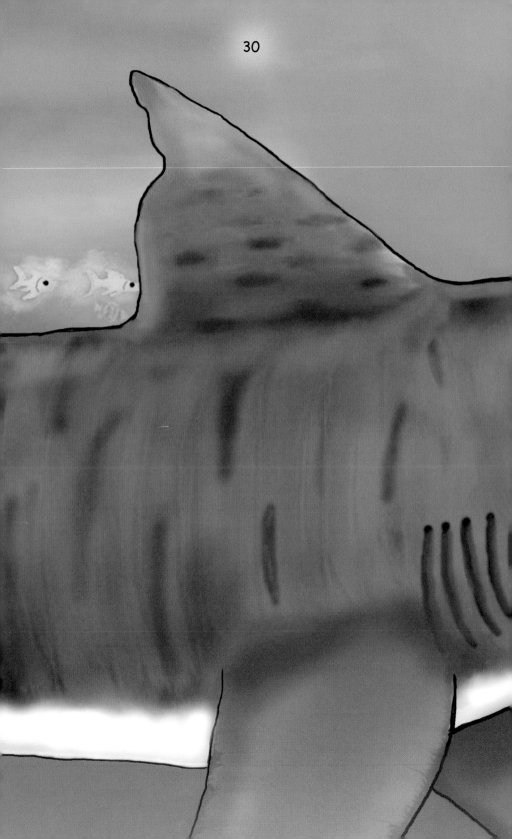

Clark could not deny the familiar face. He noticed the boy's eyes and then his lips, as they formed a smile that mouthed, "Hi!" Professor Clark knew it! It was Andrew! Clark swam very close to the diver just to make sure, when all of a sudden Clark had a brilliant idea!

After one last look at Andrew, Clark took off swimming with poor Ray hanging on, yelling and screaming, "What is going on?"

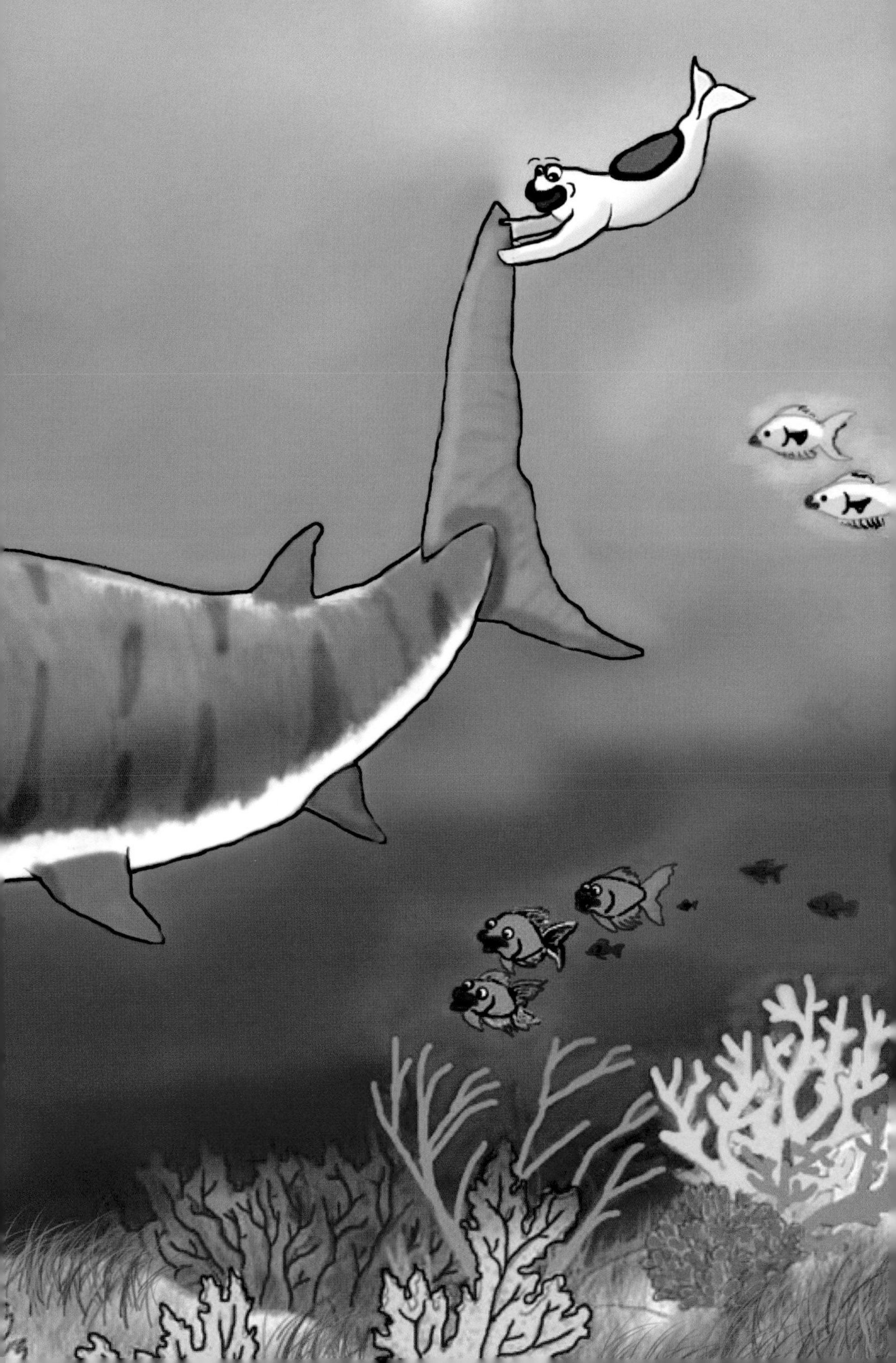

"I have to find that special lure," Clark explained to Ray, as he swam quickly to the exact spot where he first met the boy. "There it is!", shouted Ray, "Hidden in the coral, covered in brown algae and *barnacles*!"

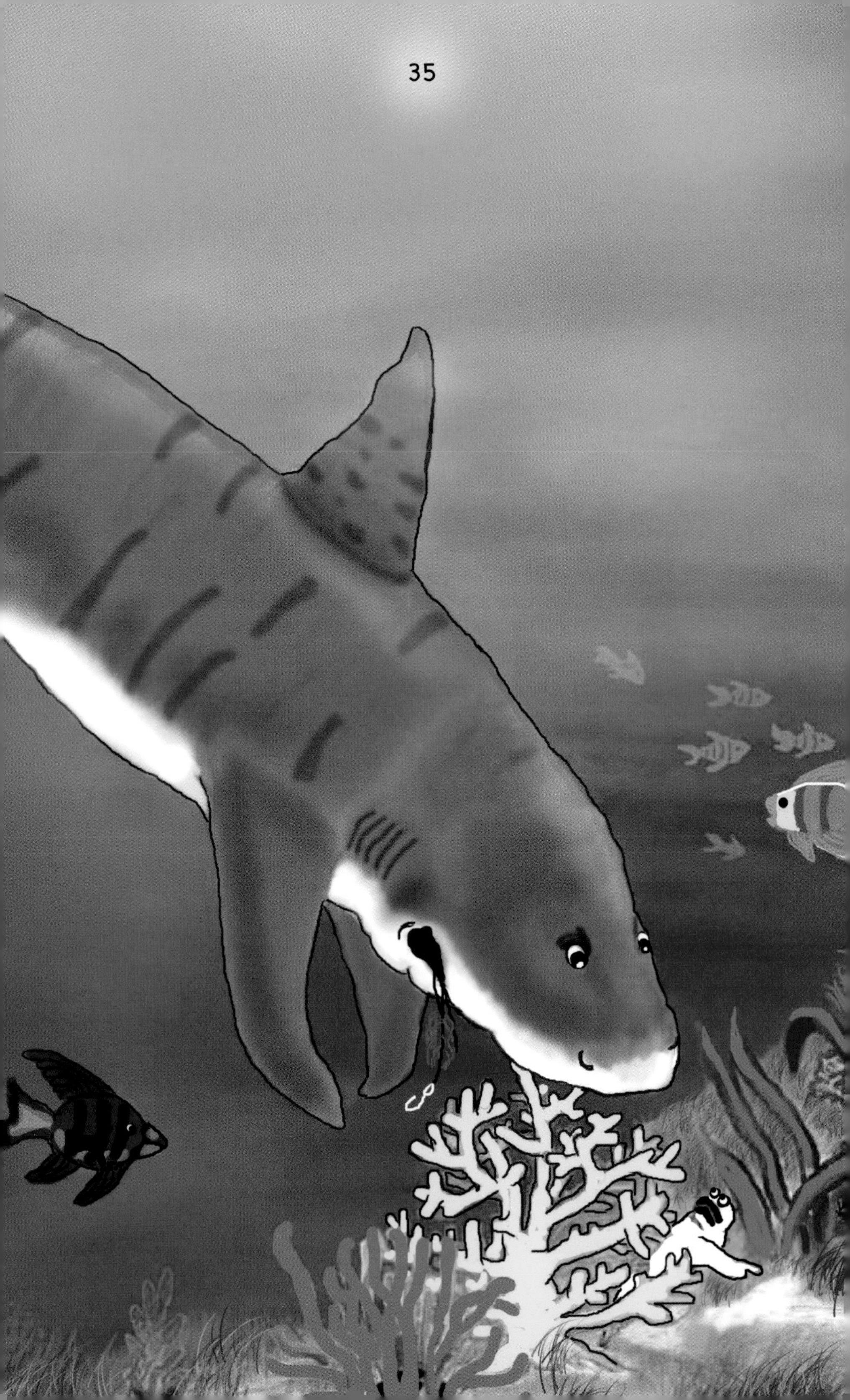

So with a gentle pull of Clark's teeth, the cherished lure was freed. Clark placed it softly in his big shark mouth, taking care not to get poked. Clark swam as fast as he could back to the divers.

Clark couldn't wait to show Andrew
that he had found his cherished lure!
Professor Clark swam right up to Andrew,
displaying the special lure secured in his
massive shark jaws!

Without hesitation, Clark gently dropped the lure into Andrew's outstretched hand.

Andrew couldn't believe it! There it was, his long-lost treasured lure, the sentimental gift from his family! He wanted to give the big, gentle shark a huge hug, but his human *instincts* reminded him that it probably wasn't a good idea.

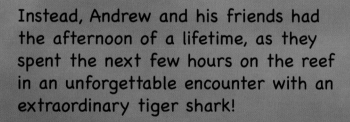

Instead, Andrew and his friends had the afternoon of a lifetime, as they spent the next few hours on the reef in an unforgettable encounter with an extraordinary tiger shark!

Clark swam around joyfully, as he was beginning to see this was the human bond he was searching for! This encounter would change Professor Clark's life forever! But how? Only time would tell.

PROFESSOR CLARK THE SCIENCE SHARK'S VOCAB LAB

RELAX:
Sharks do not sleep; instead, different parts of the brain shut down in sequence, much like sleepwalking.

REEF POLLUTION:
Coral reef pollution has become a serious problem worldwide. Scientists estimate that about twenty-five percent of the world's total coral reefs have disappeared due to a combination of pollution, overfishing, disease, and similar causes.

GULF STREAM WATERS:
A powerful, warm, and swift Atlantic Ocean current that originates at the tip of Florida and follows the eastern coastlines of the United States and Newfoundland before crossing the Atlantic Ocean.

SCUBA DIVERS:
Humans that utilize a scuba breathing device which allows them to dive and explore vast underwater environments.

MARINE ENVIRONMENT:
The areas of the world usually covered by or containing seawaters, including seas, oceans, rivers, estuaries, and coastal beaches.

ELECTRIC PULSES:
The ability to perceive natural electrical stimuli. These have been observed only in aquatic or amphibious

animals, since water is a much better conductor than air.

BARNACLES:

Small crustaceans that affix themselves to surfaces such as rocks, large sea animals, fishing lures and boats submerged in the water.

INSTINCTS:

Any behavior performed without being based upon prior experience.

Swimming through Standards

SC.K.L.14.2 - Recognize that some books and other media portray animals and plants with characteristics and behaviors they do not have in real life.

SC.K.N.1.5 Recognize that learning can come from careful observation.

SC.K.N.1.2 Make observations of the natural world and know that they are descriptors collected using the five senses.

SC.K.L.14.3 Observe plants and animals, describe how they are alike and how they are different in the way they look and in the things they do.

SC.2. N.1.1 Raise questions about the natural world, investigate them in teams through free exploration and systematic observations, and generate appropriate explanations based on those explorations.

SC.5. N.1.1, SC.3. N.1.1, SC.4. N.1.1, SC.4. N.1.6, SC.5. N.1.2, SC.5. N.1.4

SC.2. E.6.2 Describe how small pieces of rock and dead plant and animal parts can be the basis of soil and explain the process by which soil is formed.

SC.2. E.6.3 Classify soil types based on color, texture (size of particles), the ability to retain water, and the ability to support the growth of plants.

SC.2. E.7.2 Investigate by observing and measuring, that the Sun's energy directly and indirectly warms the water, land, and air.

SC.2. E.7.4 Investigate that air is all around us and that moving air is wind.

SC.2. L.16.1 Observe and describe major stages in the life cycles of plants and animals, including beans and butterflies.

SC.2. L.17.1 Compare and contrast the basic needs that all living things, including humans, have for survival.

SC.3. P.10.2 Recognize that energy has the ability to cause motion or create change.

SC.5. E.7.2 Recognize that the ocean is an integral part of the water cycle and is connected to all of Earth's water reservoirs via evaporation and precipitation processes. (assessed as SC.5. E.7.1)

SC.4. P.10.1 Observe and describe some basic forms of energy, including light, heat, sound, electrical, and the energy of motion. (assessed as SC.5. P.10.1)

SC.4. P.10.3 Investigate and explain that sound is produced by vibrating objects and that pitch depends on how fast or slow the object vibrates.

SC.4. P.10.4 Describe how moving water and air are sources of energy and can be used to move things. (assessed as SC.5. P.10.2)

SC.4. L.16.2 Explain that although characteristics of plants and animals are inherited, some characteristics can be affected by the environment. (assessed as SC.5. L.17.1)

SC.4. L.16.3 Recognize that animal behaviors may be shaped by heredity and learning. (assessed as SC.5. L.17.1)

SC.5. E.7.2 Recognize that the ocean is an integral part of the water cycle and is connected to all of Earth's water reservoirs via evaporation and precipitation processes. (assessed as SC.5. E.7.1)

SC.5. L.17.1 Compare and contrast adaptations displayed by animals and plants that enable them to survive in different environments such as life cycles variations, animal behaviors and physical characteristics. Also assessed: SC.3. L.17.1, SC.4. L.16.2, SC.4. L.16.3, SC.4. L.17.1, SC.4. L.17.4, SC.5. L.15.1

Professor Clark the Science Shark ▶ *www.ProfessorClarktheScienceShark.com*
2433 Hope Lane, Palm Beach Gardens, FL 33410